THIS MAGI BOOK BELONGS TO:

_____

UNICORN SCHOOL
238 KEW ROAD
RICHMOND
SURREY
TW9 3JX

_____

In memory of Michael Murphy
~ M.C.

For Mum and Dad
~ G.W.

Reprinted 1995, 1996, 1998

This paperback edition published 1998

First published in 1994 by Magi Publications
22 Manchester Street, London W1M 5PG

Text © 1994 Michael Coleman
Illustrations © 1994 Gwyneth Williamson

Michael Coleman and Gwyneth Williamson have
asserted their rights to be identified as the author
and illustrator of this work under the Copyright,
Designs and Patents Act, 1988.

Printed in Italy by Grafiche AZ, Verona

ISBN 1 85430 269 8

LAZY OZZIE

by
Michael Coleman

illustrated by
Gwyneth Williamson

Ozzie was a very lazy owl.

"It's time you tried
to fly," said Mother
Owl one day.
But Ozzie just said,
"Oh, do I have to?"

Ozzie didn't fancy flying one little bit.
It seemed much too much hard work,
all that wing-flapping. He just
wanted to sit around all day.
"I'm practising being wise,"
he said.

"Well, I want you
to fly," said Mother
Owl sternly. "Now, I'm going
off to look for some food. And if
you *are* wise, you will be
on the ground by the time I come back!"

Ozzie thought hard.
If he was wise, then he should be
able to think of a way of getting
down to the ground without flying.
Suddenly he noticed the horse who
lived in their barn. The horse's head
came up almost as high as the
beam Ozzie was sitting on.
Ozzie had an idea . . .

"Help, help," he yelled.
"What's the matter
with you, then?"
said the high horse.

"It's an emergency!" shouted Ozzie, jumping on to the high horse's back. "Take me to the cowshed!"

So the high horse
took Ozzie to the cowshed.

In the cowshed there lived a cow who wasn't
quite as high as the high horse.
"It's an emergency!" cried Ozzie, jumping
on to the not-quite-so-high cow's back.
"Take me to the pigsty!"

So the high horse and
the not-quite-so-high cow
took Ozzie to
the pigsty.

In the pigsty there lived a big pig.
"It's an emergency!" cried Ozzie, jumping
on to the big pig's back. "Take me to the
farmyard!"

So the high horse,
the not-quite-so-high cow
and the big pig took Ozzie
to the farmyard.

In the farmyard there lived a sheepdog.
The sheepdog wasn't as tall as the big pig.
He was a short sheepdog.
"It's an emergency!" cried Ozzie, jumping
on to the short sheepdog's back.
"Take me to the big field!"

So the high horse,
the not-quite-so-high cow,
the big pig and the short
sheepdog took Ozzie to
the big field.

In the big field there lived a little lamb.
"It's an emergency!" cried Ozzie, jumping
on to the little lamb's back. "Take me to
the duck-pond!"

So the high horse, the not-quite-so-high cow, the big pig, the short sheepdog and the little lamb took Ozzie to the duck-pond.

In the duck-pond there lived a diddy duck.
"It's an emergency!" cried Ozzie, jumping
on to the diddy duck's back. "Take me to
the barn!"

So the high horse, the not-quite-so-high cow, the big pig, the short sheepdog, the little lamb and the diddy duck took Ozzie back to the barn...

As soon as they got there, Ozzie hopped
from the diddy duck's back down
to the ground. He'd done it!
Now that's what you
call being wise,
he told himself!

"So where's the emergency?" asked the high horse.
"Ah," said Ozzie. "I was only joking. What a hoot, eh?"

The high horse, the not-quite-so-high cow,
the big pig, the short sheepdog, the little lamb
and the diddy duck weren't amused.
They all went away grumbling.
But Ozzie was pleased. His plan had worked.
He was pretty wise already.

"I flew all the way down,"
he said to Mother Owl
when she came back.

Mother Owl gave a big smile.
"Well done, son," she said.
Ozzie thought she was
pleased with him . . .

. . . but he didn't know she'd been watching all the time. "Now let me see you fly back up again," said Mother Owl.

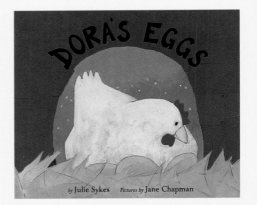

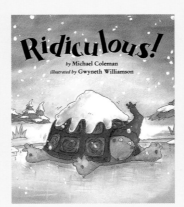
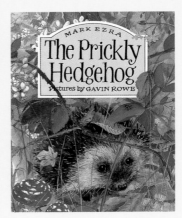

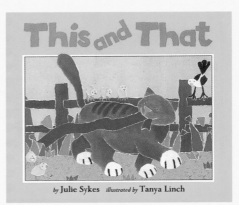